To Grace – M.K.

To Poppy Jean Pretlove, my beautiful baby girl – M.McQ xx

by Mij Kelly and

Mary McQuillan

First published in 2009 by Hodder Children's Books
First published in paperback in 2010

Text copyright © Mij Kelly 2009
Illustration copyright © Mary McQuillan 2009

Hodder Children's Books
338 Euston Road
London NW1 3BH

Hodder Children's Books Australia
Level 17/207 Kent Street
Sydney, NSW 2000

The right of Mij Kelly to be identified
as the author and Mary McQuillan as the illustrator
of this Work has been asserted by them in accordance
with the Copyright, Designs and Patents Act 1988.

A catalogue record of this book is available
from the British Library.

ISBN: 978 0 340 94526 1
10 9 8 7 6 5 4 3

Printed in China

Hodder Children's Books
is a division of Hachette
Children's Books.
An Hachette UK Company

www.hachette.co.uk

AtchoO!

MIJ KELLY   MARY McQUILLAN

*Hodder
Children's
Books*

A division of Hachette Children's Books

This is the story of Suzy Sue
and the fateful day
when she went…

Her friends, who knew all
the social graces and didn't like
germs being spat in their faces,
cried,

'Suzy Sue!
Please!
Please!
Please!
Cover your mouth
if you're going
to sneeze!'

'I'm ever-so-sorry,'
said Suzy Sue.
'I just didn't know
that's what I should do.'

Well that raised a rumpus…

'It's true,' said the cow.
'She is **horribly** rude,
but that **doesn't** mean
she can't
be improved.

If we teach her the **rules,**
I'm sure we can
save her from
a life of bad
manners
and ghastly
behaviour.'

Good
Manners
For
Complete
Animals

Rule Number 1 is don't be disgusting.

'Well look whose **manners** need adjusting!'

'This dog is doing things all **wrong.** He's **grotty,** he's **snotty** and, **boy,** does he **pong!**'

'Take a **bath** and **brush** your teeth.
Learn to use a **handkerchief**.
If you've got a **runny** nose,
please don't wipe it
on your clothes!'

Rule Number 2 is don't eat like a pig.

'Look at them slurping. They don't care a fig.
Surely they know it's **revolting**
and **rude** to wallow about like
that in your food.'

'Wash your hands before you eat.
Don't **stand** in your dinner. **Sit** in your seat.
Try not to burp and **whatever** you do,
keep your mouth **shut** when you chew!'

Rule Number 3 is do not fight.

'Some people can't tell what's
wrong from what's right.
Just look at these cats!
They lack poise.
They lack charm.
They're a social disaster,
a disgrace to the farm!'

'Say please and thank you.
Always play fair.
And whatever you do,

SHARE!
SHARE!
SHARE!'

'That's it,' said the cow.
'Those are the **rules**.
Three **pearls** of wisdom,
absolute **jewels**.'

'Don't
pong like
a dog!

Or

eat like a pig.

Don't fight like a cat –

it's not clever or big!'

The cats and pigs were up in arms.
So were their friends from other farms.

'They spoilt our game of tug-of-war!'

'We don't like them any more!'

'They ruined our meal!'

'They made us cry!'

Down with Sheep!

Cows are rude!

We're in a very angry mood!

'I don't really smell... do I?'

'Look what you've done,' said Suzy Sue,
'Your friends are **really** mad with you.
You hurt their feelings. You were cruel.
You broke the most important rule.'

The *golden rule* is always do
what you'd like others to do to you.

'That means **be kind**,' said Suzy Sue.
'Remember they've got feelings too.'

'When you told me I smelt bad, you made me feel really sad.'

'Oh darn!' said the sheep. 'We can't tell the dog he's a horrible, stinky, mangy old slob.'

'But maybe we can give him hints – like bubble bath, or peppermints.'

Good Manners For Complete Animals

'If you're kind,' said Suzy Sue,
'people sometimes learn from you.'

'You pushed me about.
Don't you see?
You can't teach me
manners by bullying me.'

Cows are rude!

'Botheration!'
said
the
horse.

'We can't
make pigs
change by using force.

But if we make sure
that we're polite, they'll copy us
and get it right.'

'If you're kind,' said Suzy Sue,
'people will be kind to you.'

'You chopped our tug-of-war
in two. We never want
to speak to you.'

'Oh dear,' said the goat,
'we made a mistake – though
with cats such mistakes
are easy to make!'

'But if we're
sorry and
make amends,
maybe…

…we can all be friends!'

After that, things were
sweetness and light.
They all helped each
other to be **polite.**

The pigs sipped from tea cups.
The dog took a shower.
The cats skipped around
handing out flowers.

And when they gave one to Suzy Sue –

A A A...

'Would you like a hanky?'

'Yes, thank you.'

'You'd **never** believe she was born in a zoo!'

Suzy Sue – 6 months